CHRISTMAS AT THE INN

MAIL ORDER BRIDES OF SHADOW GULCH

SUSANNAH CALLOWAY

Tica House
Publishing

Sweet Romance that Delights and Enchants!

PERSONAL WORD FROM THE AUTHOR

Dearest Readers,

Thank you so much for choosing one of my books. I am proud to be a part of the team of writers at Tica House Publishing who work joyfully to bring you stories of hope, faith, courage, and love. Your kind words and loving readership are deeply appreciated.

I would like to personally invite you to sign up for updates and to become part of our **Exclusive Reader Club**—it's completely Free to join! We'd love to welcome you!

Much love,

Susannah Calloway

VISIT HERE to Join our Reader's Club and to Receive Tica House Updates!

https://wesrom.subscribemenow.com/

CONTENTS

Personal Word From The Author   1
Chapter 1   4
Chapter 2   12
Chapter 3   25
Chapter 4   32
Chapter 5   39
Chapter 6   48
Chapter 7   56
Chapter 8   62
Chapter 9   70
Chapter 10   83
Chapter 11   91
Continue Reading…   94
Thanks For Reading!   97

More Mail Order Bride Romances for You!   99
About the Author   101

The day that Rebecca Vanderhall learned of her inevitable fate dawned cold and bright. The brilliant sunlight and the achingly clear blue skies were a stark contrast to the darkness of the future that she now knew awaited her.

Her father, seated at the head of the table and wearing his usual three-piece suit and thunderous scowl, relayed the news to her with utmost calm.

She would have expected nothing less from him.

Still, his pronouncement felt like a slap to the face as she was faced with the reality, the unchangeableness of his words.

Numbly, she repeated his words. "I'm to marry – and I am betrothed to Mr. Reginald Rogers."

Vaughn Vanderhall gave a single nod. She should not push her luck any further; her father did not appreciate being questioned. But she couldn't quite keep herself from speaking out once more.

"But Father, I don't want to marry him."

His brows drew down even further over his hawklike nose. "Why not, pray tell? Have you something against the holy arrangement of matrimony?"

"Well, no," she managed. Truthfully, she had often secretly dreamed of marrying someone – preferably someone who lived thousands of miles away, someone who swept her off her feet and carried her off into the sunset without so much as asking permission to court her – or a second glance.

"Then what could possibly be your objection? He's a fine, upstanding young man. You know he is my particular protégé – when I look at that young man, I see myself, thirty years ago."

Becky bit her lip. That was exactly the problem; Reginald Rogers was the spitting image of her father. The idea of being tied to him for life was enough to make her cry.

But she couldn't cry here, not in front of her father, who was taking her silence as a sign that her objection had been forcefully overcome.

As well he might. Becky was an unmarried woman of twenty-one, still living under her father's roof, and in the eyes of society, he had every right to make arrangements for her marriage. In theory, a marriage was to provide for her care and keeping; thinking of what Rogers might be like as a husband, on the other hand, gave her the shudders. As she had seen her father cow and belittle her mother the entire time that she was growing up, she could only imagine that his protégé would learn from his example.

What was it with men? she wondered sometimes. They mystified her. Their preacher had stated more than once from the pulpit that men were given authority so as to protect the women in their charge, but she certainly had not seen that in action…

She slid her gaze toward her mother, seeking for any response. She knew better than to expect a verbal objection; she couldn't remember the last time her poor mother had dared open her mouth against her husband's wishes.

Gertrude Llewellyn Vanderhall was descended from the Long Island Llewellyns, with a family history as wealthy as the kings of England. But somewhere along the way, she had been taken in by the handsome features and the "all hail the conquering hero" attitude of Vaughn Vanderhall, the son of a merchant who had struck it rich in the early 1830s. He had brought up his son to believe that the world was owed to him. Perhaps that arrogance had been charming when Vaughn Vanderhall was young, but coming from a man in his fifties, with half of Boston bowing and scraping at his feet, it was distinctly off-putting, to say the least.

Even now, Becky's mother was still strikingly pretty. The fair skin, the wide violet-blue eyes and blonde ringlets that had originally attracted her suitor were still in evidence. But there were shadows under those wide eyes, and lines of sadness around her mouth. At barely forty, her hair was prematurely scattered with silver gray.

Becky knew her mother's best features had been handed down to her daughter, but she was rather indifferent to her own looks. They hadn't brought her much other than unwanted attention from men like Reginald Rogers.

She only just prevented herself from saying, "How long do I have left?"

Instead, the question was phrased a bit more diplomatically – "When have you scheduled the wedding?"

Her father took this as acknowledgement that she would bow to his wishes, as everyone inevitably did. The corner of his mouth turned up, the closest thing he ever got to a smile.

"You'll be married by Christmas. The exact date will be communicated to you as the details are decided. But you will begin the new year as Mrs. Rogers."

Becky clamped her jaw tightly, fighting against the flood of words that were battling to escape. She saw her future in front of her, a lifetime of silence and depression, gradually withdrawing into herself until there was nothing of her left…

Her eyes were drawn once again to her mother, who was looking at her plate and not meeting her gaze.

A lifetime spent like that of her mother…

The words that now came to her mind were not of anger, but of despair.

How she made it through the rest of the dinner, she was never quite sure. But once her father finally dismissed them and retired to his study to contemplate his post-dinner brandy, she caught her mother by the elbow as she walked toward the sitting room.

"Mother, can I speak with you?"

Her mother hesitated, then nodded. She couldn't help but suspect that Becky wanted to speak of the impending nuptials, of course; she was subdued and defeated, but she wasn't ignorant. In her hesitation, Becky could read her mother's reluctance to be asked to interfere, but her love for her daughter won out.

They settled close together in the sitting room, feet in front of the fire. Becky sat with the door in her peripheral vision, in case her father decided to enter abruptly.

"Mother," she said, her voice low and urgent, "you must know what I want to ask you."

"Oh, my dear." Gertrude Vanderhall sighed, touching a finger to the line of worry between her thin brows. "You know I cannot interfere with your father's plans. It's a matter of business."

"How can it be a matter of business? It's my life. And besides, I don't see how it will help his business. Mr. Rogers is his employee, after all."

"Your father prefers the word associate, dear. Yes, Mr. Rogers is subordinate – but it's traditional for a man in his position to marry into the family, especially as he will likely be taking over the business when your father chooses to retire."

Becky knew that it was uncouth, but she couldn't help but snort derisively.

"As if Father would ever retire," she said. "He couldn't bear to give up the chance to tell everyone what to do and lord it over all he sees."

"Rebecca."

"You know that I'm right, Mother. He thrives on it – everyone and everything around him must remain absolutely submissive to him or he simply won't be able to function. Why, if you or I ever broke away from his iron grasp, he wouldn't know what to do with himself."

Her mother shook her head. "Darling, you know what he would say if he heard you speak like this."

"Well, I'll keep it to just us, then," said Becky. "But it isn't as if I haven't thought about outright telling him."

Her mother reached out and put a hand on hers, smiling a bit sadly.

"I know it's very difficult. But he is your father, dear, and he does the best he can to provide for you. I'm sure that's the real motive for everything that he does."

Becky had her doubts about this. As far as she could tell, her father had never done a single thing that wasn't in his own interests. If it happened to benefit his family, well, that was a side effect, and not a necessary one by any means.

But her words about breaking free of his grasp – and her vivid imagining of what he would do once he found out – had stirred something in her. With the prospect of marrying Reginald Rogers looming with certainty in front of her, she felt more determined than she had ever been before to simply not let her father's plans come to fruition. How she would go about preventing them was another task entirely; but it was daring enough to seriously consider making it happen.

All her life, she had been prone to wayward thoughts centering on escaping her father's home, making her own decisions, living her own life. But she had feared that her secret thoughts would be written on her face for all to see and feared that punishment would follow swiftly. His plans had never been so disastrous to her that they were worse than the consequences of disobedience...until now.

She absolutely could not face the idea of actually joining her life to a man like Reginald Rogers.

Her mother was facing the fire again, her thin hands rubbing slowly back and forth as she sought warmth. Becky felt overcome with affection for her poor mother; she had done her best to raise her only daughter to know love and safety, though her efforts had been severely hindered by her husband. Why, Gertrude Llewellyn was younger than Becky was now when she became a bride. Practically a child. She hadn't had the faintest idea what she was getting into, and Vaughn Vanderhall had molded her as he wanted. A quiet, mild creature who wouldn't say boo to a goose – but a woman who carried a deep respect for her husband, and a deep love for her daughter.

Whatever happened, Becky promised herself, she wouldn't leave her mother behind. She would have to bring her along. But what could she do?

She lapsed into furious thought, wracking her brains for ideas, acutely conscious that it was growing ever closer to December and the Christmas season – and painfully aware that her time was already running short.

CHAPTER 2

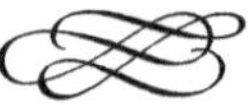

On the day that Rebecca Vanderhall began to see the light at the end of the tunnel, it was cold and blustery outside, with charcoal clouds hovering low over the city and the sun hiding far away.

Her mother was ankle-deep in preparations for the upcoming Christmas party. The Vanderhall house hosted the company dinner each year, with the more important members of Vanderhall Incorporated in attendance, their well-dressed wives on their arms. Though it was still some four weeks away, there was already much to be done. Wreaths and garlands to be ordered, the tree to be decorated, the menu set, and supplies called for. Boston was a city of rich and seemingly endless celebrations, and the makings for the best of parties were in high demand.

Rebecca would rather have avoided the whole thing. It was her father's one concession to humanity, in her opinion, and his enthusiasm for the Christmas holiday struck her as nothing more than hypocrisy rivaling that of the Pharisees.

At the same time, though, it was a chance to spend time with her mother when Gertrude got so caught up in her tasks that she actually seemed enlivened, cheerful, almost happy.

And so, Rebecca set aside her needlepoint and joined in gladly enough when her mother asked for help to set the menu.

They sat around the kitchen with the cook, discussing options and the necessary supplies, drinking hot cocoa and basking in the warmth of the fire while the frigid late November wind howled outside. It was a pleasant enough way to spend the day, and Becky found herself relaxing more than she would have expected as her mother and the cook discussed the best way of stuffing a goose versus offering the guests ham. Becky had a feeling that it would end in them deciding to order both; it usually did.

There was rarely a large crowd at the sort of parties that were hosted at the Vanderhalls, but they were filled with only the best people – the sort of people, at least, that Vaughn Vanderhall considered to qualify as "best." Becky knew that she shouldn't be so dismissive of strangers simply because they fit into her father's ideal social mold, but it was difficult to remember at times, and she certainly wasn't looking forward to the dinner.

She liked Christmas time, apart from that. When the snow fell, Boston took on a clean, fresh look that made her think of starting over, starting new. Sometimes, when she was unable to sleep, she would sit up at her window during the night and watch the flakes swirl down to the ground, dreaming of having her own new world…

Her mother and the cook were still deep in conversation. Idly, Becky reached for the newspaper that sat on one corner of the table, where the cook or one of the maids had been reading it during their tea break. She did not often read the paper; her father frowned on the practice of a young woman taking an interest in the world, thus he usually kept the upstairs paper in his study. But down here, in the midst of the servants' world, there were no such obstructions, and she could read freely. Her mother didn't even notice when she picked it up.

She was paging through the articles when the advertisement on the back page caught her eye.

Seeking adventurous young women.

She couldn't help but look at it a little more closely. When she saw the words matrimonial agency, she sucked in a breath and darted a swift glance up at the others. But neither her mother nor the cook was paying her any attention; both of them were now pouring over hastily hand-written dessert menus. Becky returned her attention to the paper and read the words almost greedily.

Seeking adventurous young women. Are you an unmarried, unattached female between the ages of eighteen and thirty? Do you have a yearning for excitement, romance, and adventure? McKay's Matrimonial Agency has brought many a happy couple together. We have several respectable bachelors just waiting to be matched with a suitable wife. Fill out an application today.

Below that, was the street address for McKay's. It was several blocks from the Vanderhall house, but Becky knew the general area. She moved to tear the slip of paper from the page and then stopped, glancing up again at her mother. No, she would have to present her with a *fait accompli*; she couldn't risk her finding out about it beforehand and telling her father. He would be sure to find a way to block her from seeking out the agency; though it seemed ludicrous that a young woman her age would be so under the thumb of her parent, she knew full well that Vaughn Vanderhall was not above locking her in her bedroom for weeks at a time.

But her memory was good, and she read over the address several times, mouthing it soundlessly to herself to imprint it on her memory.

The rest of the morning seemed to crawl by, though her mother continually turned to her and asked for her input, evidently seeing that Becky was not entirely engrossed in the proceedings. Most of the menu had been decided upon, apart from a few details that needed mulling over, by the time Becky and Gertrude ascended the stairs from the kitchen and found themselves on the main first floor once again.

"Well, dear," said Gertrude with a faint smile, "I do hope that your father is pleased with the decisions that we have made today."

"As long as it impresses his associates, I'm sure he will be," Becky said.

"Hmm – there's only a few hours yet until it's time to get ready for dinner. Should we tackle the question of decorations next, or let that be for another day?"

Becky seized her opportunity with both hands.

"Honestly, Mother, I think it's best left until tomorrow. You know how flustered you tend to get if we try to fit too much into a single day. Besides, if you settle all the questions of how Christmas is supposed to be decorated, what will you do until the day itself finally arrives?"

She smiled and put her arm around her mother's waist. "I think that you've earned yourself an early afternoon nap. Besides, it's the perfect weather for it."

"Well, perhaps you're right, dear – and that way I'll be freshened up and ready when your father arrives home from work. What will you do?"

"Oh, I think I might take a walk – just a short one, not too far." Comparatively speaking, she added to herself, guilty at the little white lie she was telling. But it was necessary – and besides, it would be for the good of her mother as well as for herself, if everything went according to plan.

Her mother raised her eyebrows. "A walk? On a day that was so tailor-made for a nap?"

"A nice brisk walk, and then a nap afterwards. I'm feeling fidgety, Mother, and you know how Father hates it when I can't sit still at the dinner table."

"Yes, he does dislike his dinner being disrupted." Gertrude put a hand on Becky's cheek. "Well, then, please be careful, dear. And don't stay gone too late."

"I won't, Mother."

She walked upstairs alongside her mother and then watched as Gertrude closed herself into her room. Then she was into her own room in a flash, finding her boots, pulling a coat and hat down from the wardrobe so quickly that she knocked off the cedar hangers, and putting herself together as rapidly as she could.

Then she was back downstairs, pausing to look out the window next to the front door on the off chance that her father had decided to come home early. But it was still two and a half hours before he was due back, and she breathed a prayer that he would stick to his schedule, as he was so inclined to do.

It didn't take her as long as she feared to make it to the matrimonial agency, and there was almost no one in the little lobby of the office, which was both gratifying and a bit worrisome. Surely, she couldn't be the only one who had seen the advertisement – surely, she couldn't be the only adventuresome girl in Boston.

On the other hand, she told herself, it was entirely possible she was the only one who desperately wanted to be married and out of Boston well before Christmas.

Not everyone had a father quite like hers, after all…

Whatever the case, there was only one young woman waiting ahead of her, and she was called back to a desk at the back of the room shortly after Becky's arrival. Becky smiled at the receptionist, who smiled back and said, "It will be just a few moments."

How those few moments crawled by. She was so anxious she could hardly stand it.

But by the time the other girl had left, and Becky was called back herself, only an hour had passed since she'd left the house. She still had an hour and a half before the earliest time that her father would arrive home, and she breathed a sigh of relief as she sank into the chair across from the agent.

The questions were brief and to the point. Name, age, and marital status. Any outstanding obligations or arrangements – "Meaning are you betrothed to anyone," the agent clarified, looking at Becky over the top of her half-moon glasses.

Becky swallowed hard past the lump in her throat. But it wasn't a lie, after all – she certainly hadn't agreed to marry Reginald Roberts, no matter what her father said.

"No," she said, staunchly. "I have no engagements."

"And no family members who are dependent on you?"

Should she mention her mother? No, surely that would be a bad idea; it might make it more difficult for her to find a match if the agent thought that she had someone dependent on her. And her mother wasn't dependent, not really – though Becky fully intended to drag her along with her, regardless.

"No, none."

"What do your parents say about your decision to apply, Miss Vanderhall?"

For the third time in as many minutes, she faced the moment of truth. But this time she could not in good conscience hide anything from the agent.

"They don't know about it," she admitted. "And I have a feeling that they would not approve – but I am twenty-one years old, ma'am, and I know my own mind. I don't mind if they cast me off without a penny. I've got to get out before – I've got to go and do something with my life. And I simply cannot do it here. I need a new start."

The agent eyed her stiffly for a moment, and then seemed to relax. Something like a smile even showed on her face.

"If I've heard it once, I've heard it a million times," she said. "I don't blame you one bit, Miss Vanderhall. Well, you're a grown woman, and your secret is safe with McKay's Matrimonial Agency. But for the sake of your peace of mind, I urge you not to burn any bridges between yourself and your parents if you can help it. At the very least, write them a letter after you arrive and let them know that you are safe and sound. Trust me – I speak from experience."

Becky nodded. "Very well," she said. "I appreciate your understanding – and your discretion."

The agent stamped the page she had been writing on, set it in a file folder, and then turned her attention to a drawer full of papers. She shuffled through them for a moment, and then pulled one out and squinted at it.

"When can you leave?"

"As soon as I pack my things."

"You don't mind travel?"

"I relish it."

"Then I think I've found your match." She set the paper down and slid it across the desk to Becky, who picked it up, blinking at the suddenness of it.

"Already?"

The agent nodded. "This is the reason why we posted the advertisement that you answered – there are far more lonely bachelors than there are eligible young women, evidently. We have quite a backlog. But this fellow has been waiting for several months, and I think it's quite time to put him out of his misery, don't you?"

Becky read over the paper swiftly, feeling her heart do double-jumps in her chest and butterflies spread nervous wings in her middle. The name of her husband-to-be was Walter Adams, aged thirty-two. He was a well-heeled rancher outside of a town called Shadow Gulch, Idaho, which was reachable only by stagecoach. In his letter of application, he accounted for himself as being tall and thin, with dark hair and brown eyes. He was a widower of three years but did not give any other details about his story, nor did he waste time describing the loneliness that had driven him to write for a Mail Order Bride. He didn't mince words, nor did he describe himself or his surroundings in romantic or poetic terms.

Becky considered this and decided she liked it. A straightforward man was to be prized, she told herself; it was when they started getting all romantic and moon-eyed that life became unbearable.

Of course, she had little enough experience with such things herself, but she told herself very sternly that she much preferred an unromantic man.

"Shall I write to him?" she asked, looking up again. "To let him know that I'm coming?"

"You won't have time if you intend to leave right away. We'll send him a telegram."

"All right – is there anything else?"

"One more thing, Miss Vanderhall." The agent gave another rare smile. "Go and enjoy your new start."

Becky smiled back, feeling elation start in the pit of her stomach and work its way gradually upward. "Thank you," she said. "I intend to."

She carried the knowledge of her new plans with her all the way back to the house, and she kept them close in mind during dinner time. Her father was in rare form, outlining plans for the wedding and how he intended to use the occasion to further his position with some merchants who would almost certainly attend. He appeared more determined than ever to make the most of every opportunity to expand his business. His casual mercenary air would usually have been upsetting to Becky, if not downright incendiary; but with every statement about his plans, she thought something along the lines of, "I hope you can still have a wedding without a bride," and, "If you're that excited about it, perhaps you should marry Reginald Rogers yourself."

She almost got in trouble at this last thought and tried to hide a smile by taking a sip of water. But her father caught it and narrowed his eyes at her.

"What's that smirk on your face, my girl?"

"Nothing, Father, I just got a bit of something caught in my throat."

"Are you certain?"

It took all she had to face him with wide and guileless eyes and tell him that yes, she was absolutely certain. But it was true, though all the details were not told – she was absolutely certain she did not want to explain to him exactly what she had been thinking.

Under the guise of going for another walk the next day, she managed to slip out and make her way to the train station. It was farther away than the matrimonial agency, in the opposite direction in a less-affluent part of town, and she hurried as quickly as possible through the cold November morning, her thick coat wrapped tightly around her and her low heels clicking on the tightly-joined cobbles.

But her errand was completed hastily, and the ticket master did not even give her a second glance as he handed over the two slips of paper. Her heart was thrumming a hundred miles a minute as she turned and made her way back to the house.

Well, she'd done it. She'd bought the tickets, and the train would be waiting for her the very next morning. She had only one more day to get through – one more day to hide her plans from her father…

One more day to figure out how to get her mother on the train alongside her.

CHAPTER 3

Taking her mother with her was the biggest sticking point. As desperate as Rebecca was to get away, she could not in good conscience see leaving her poor mother to face the brunt of Vaughn Vanderhall's displeasure alone. Besides, it seemed that each year Gertrude Vanderhall lost a little bit more of herself; in another few years, would anything be left?

No, Rebecca had to manage it. But how?

She spent a sleepless night wracking her brains over what could be done about the situation and rose the next morning with determination. Her mother would never consent to coming with her if she knew the plan. Despite how badly she had been treated by her husband, her loyalty was to the sanctity of marriage – admirable, but misguided in this instance, in Becky's opinion. The only option was outright trickery.

With that in mind, she packed her small bag with as many necessities as she could manage and tucked in the allowance money she'd been stowing away for the last few years. If nothing else, they could purchase whatever they needed in terms of clothing and food along the way. With that done, she stood for a moment and looked around her room – but there was nothing here that she regretted leaving behind very much.

The time had come.

She put on her best boots and her warmest coat, took up her hat and gloves, and went to her mother's bedroom door.

Gertrude Vanderhall was seated at her writing desk in the corner, finishing up the last of the invitations for the Christmas dinner. She looked up at her daughter's arrival and smiled.

"Hello, dear. What are you up to this morning?"

"I'd very much like to go for a walk, Mother, but I wondered – would you go with me?"

Gertrude put down her pen.

"Well, I am terribly busy this morning…"

"I have a secret," Becky blurted out. "I walked down Atlantic Avenue yesterday, just to see what that part of town was like, and I came across this poor woman – she's in awful shape, Mother. Her husband is horribly cruel. Her daughter is in despair, not knowing what to do to help her mother. I'm afraid that if I don't do something, she'll slip away into oblivion, and no one will ever know what's become of her."

Her mother's face was a picture of worry, with sympathy for the unknown woman written large. "Oh, the poor dear."

"I told them I would return this morning, but I thought you would know best what to do for her. Would you go with me?"

"Of course, I will, dear. Let me get my coat."

"It's best to bundle up," Becky said, handing her the warmest clothing her mother owned. Her heart was beating quickly again, seeing triumph on the horizon but still worried everything could crash to a halt with one misstep, one wrong word, or her father's sudden arrival early from work. "And…" A bright idea crossed her mind. "This poor woman is so badly taken care of, she lacks everything – would you take a dress or two for her? She's about your size."

Gertrude stopped what she was doing and put a hand on Becky's cheek, smiling at her fondly.

"Oh, my dear, I do love your kind instincts. Of course, I will. Shall we take some food?"

"I'll run downstairs and have them make up a packet."

Run downstairs? She fairly flew. Once she had given orders in the kitchen, she raced back upstairs and found a larger handbag, throwing an extra dress and nightclothes into it. Her mother's "donation" clothing would just fit on top, and then they would have only the one bag to take along with them.

Now that Gertrude realized what Becky was so intent upon, her enthusiasm picked up a bit for the outing. She was not very strong, and Becky knew she would need more time to walk to the train station than Becky herself required. Time was an issue, but with hurrying and coaxing, she managed to get herself and her mother out onto the street, with bag and packet of food in hand, heading in the right direction. She couldn't help but glance back at the three-story house in which she had grown up – God willing, it would be the last time she saw it. She was filled with an intense satisfaction at the thought of leaving it behind.

"What is it, dear?" her mother prompted. "Have you forgotten something?"

Becky turned back to face the way ahead.

"No," she said, and put her arm through her mother's, squeezing it against her side and smiling. "I've got everything I need."

The last and most difficult part of the leave-taking came as they moved into sight of the train station.

"Does your new friend live around here somewhere?" Gertrude looked about them, thoughtfully. It was a highly industrial area, and unlikely that anyone would have a home there.

"I'm to meet her at the station," Becky said, hurrying Gertrude along with her. The train was waiting, already puffing, and she heard the whistle blow once, twice.

Gertrude came along without complaining, though Becky could see she was puzzled. They made it to the station, with the train just a few feet away and ready to leave.

"Rebecca – what's going on?"

Becky turned to face her mother, slowly. She took the tickets from her pocket and held them up.

"I'm sorry," she said, "I haven't been entirely truthful with you. I've bought us tickets for this train. It will take us west – to meet my husband-to-be in Idaho. I've applied to become a Mail Order Bride because I simply will not marry Reginald Rogers. I must get away from Father because I know he won't take no for an answer. I need to start over again – and I believe that you do, too."

She made her words as gentle as possible, trying to explain as quickly as she could, knowing there was no way her mother could take it all in. If only she could get her onto the train and explain there.

But her mother's puzzled frown had only deepened. "Is there no unfortunate woman, then?"

"Oh, Mother." Becky took Gertrude's hand and squeezed it, looking into her eyes searchingly. "You are the unfortunate woman. You've been ill-used and treated cruelly and denied love for far too long. You're fading away before my very eyes. I cannot leave you here with Father, but I cannot stay here, either. You must come with me."

Gertrude took in a shuddering breath. "Rebecca, I don't…"

The train whistled again, and a porter called out from the door, "All aboard."

"Come on, Mother, we can talk on the train."

"Rebecca."

"If you change your mind," Becky said rashly, "I'll send you back again. Truly, I will. But I don't think you'll change your mind." She took her mother's arm and hustled her toward the train. "Come on, we'll miss it."

For a split second, she thought her mother would resist, and despaired. She couldn't force her to get on the train… Indeed, if her mother truly did not want to go, she wouldn't force her. For wouldn't that be as bad as what her father was trying to do to her?

Becky realized right there and then that she would have to accept it if her mother refused to go. But then it occurred to her that her mother was moving along with her, not entirely willingly, but moving forward. Her heart soared.

Three steps up and they were on the train, which was already moving. The station, and the rest of their lives in Boston, were steadily being left behind.

CHAPTER 4

The journey west was by no means easy – nor was it accomplished in a matter of a few days. It was freezing cold the entire way, and Becky was grateful she'd had the foresight to ensure they both wore their warmest coats, as well as hats, gloves, and scarves. A landslide had occurred on the tracks a few days before, and there was a delay while the work crew completed the clearing of it.

Worst of all was the moment she realized, stepping off the train in Philadelphia, that her father had somehow gotten wind of what was going on, and had sent men to look for them.

She couldn't explain how she knew it was her father's work – but she did, deep down in her soul. The men were plainly and drably dressed, but they were on the platform as though waiting, searching the faces of each and every person who came down from the train. She knew in her heart they were detectives, Pinkertons, there to find her and her mother and force them to return to Boston to face her father's wrath.

Fear clutched at her heart, and she breathed a frantic prayer, at a loss for what to do. How could they slip out without being noticed?

Whether it was an answer to her prayer or not, the fight that broke out at the far end of the station platform provided exactly the distraction that was needed. The two men hesitated, and then, as there were shouts and calls for the police, ran in that direction. Evidently, they felt a higher responsibility to law and order than simply finding a runaway housewife and her adult daughter, Becky thought, practically giddy with the timing of it all. She took her mother by the arm and slipped down the stairs to the ground, making it out of the station before the sounds of the scuffle faded away into the distance.

With that close call behind them, they set off on the next part of their long journey: travel by stagecoach.

As they went farther and farther away from the east, Becky began to breathe a little easier. Her father couldn't possibly know where she was headed, and he would expect her to stick to the railways, not change to a stage. There seemed so little likelihood of him discovering her whereabouts or her destination that she even felt bold enough to send a telegram on one overnight stop, to let him know she and her mother were safe and well.

That satisfied the suggestion of the agent in the office, she thought, to contact the parent at home.

Her mother – well, her mother was another issue entirely.

Gertrude Vanderhall was not at all sure about the journey she was undertaking, and from the moment they set foot on the train, Becky was worried that her mother would simply bolt and head back on the next train to Boston. But though she was clearly brimming with nervous energy, even wringing her hands at times, she sat and listened to Becky's explanation: her decision to escape the arranged marriage, her interview with the agent, her certainty that she could not leave her mother behind.

"And you must know that I care for you and that I believe this will be for the best," Becky finished up quietly. "You must feel it yourself – Father has always been difficult, but he's been worse these last few years. Sometimes I fear for your safety."

Her mother nodded slowly. "Yes," she said softly—almost in a whisper. "You're right. I've tried to speak to him about it – I believe he is too preoccupied with his work. He … loses sight of what's right…"

"That doesn't excuse the fact that he treats his family so badly," Becky pointed out. "We are not commodities to be used as he sees fit. I am not willing to trade my future so that he feels secure in how long his business will last."

"I-I know you're right, dear," Gertrude admitted, her expression deeply sad. "He is wrong to try and force you to marry – and I'm sorry that you have been driven to this rash action. But Rebecca…to marry a complete stranger… You don't know that this man will be any better than Mr. Rogers, and he may be worse."

Becky bit her lip.

"Maybe," she said. "But I have to hope. And if we arrive there and things go badly, well – we'll start over again. Now that we've done it once, we can surely handle it a second time."

Gertrude shook her head.

"I don't think I should be here," she said softly. "If it weren't for my concern for you, my only child, I would be on my way back to Boston."

Becky clutched her hand.

"Please stay with me," she pleaded. "Please say you'll stay – at least until the marriage is done with and I'm settled. Give it that long at least."

It was clear that Gertrude wasn't happy about her daughter's request, but she nodded acquiescence. And, Becky hoped, perhaps once they arrived in Shadow Gulch, she would change her mind and stay.

On they went through the darkening winter, with snow one day and sleet the next, keeping each other's spirits up by speaking of the future to come. Becky's biggest misstep was in mentioning the Christmas season that was almost upon them; she saw the change in her mother's face instantly and knew she was thinking of the Christmas preparations she had left undone.

Becky reached out to take her mother's hand.

"But we'll be celebrating in a new place this year," she said. "And with my husband, to boot. Think how exciting it will be, Mother – I hear that Idaho has evergreens growing in little unexpected forests, here and there. It will be as though there are Christmas trees everywhere around us."

At her cheerful words, she was glad to see her mother rally.

Still, the journey was difficult. When they finally arrived at their last stop, they were both thoroughly relieved.

The stagecoach rumbled into Shadow Gulch on dirt roads packed into hard mud by the cold wind. It was mid-afternoon, and the sun was headed swiftly for the horizon. Becky stepped out of the coach first and helped her mother down. A porter tossed her bag down from where it was strapped on the roof, and she caught it handily, holding tightly to it with one hand and to her mother's arm with the other. Thus fortified, she felt ready to look around her and try to find her husband-to-be.

But there was no one there that looked as though he could possibly be Walter Adams.

She led her mother toward the wooden sidewalk, peering up and down the wide street into the gathering gloom. Still there was no one except a few disinterested passers-by, and her heart sank. She could tell, glancing at her mother, that Gertrude was no less concerned.

"Here, miss, are you Becky Vanderhall?" the porter called over to them.

She stepped toward him. "Yes, that's me."

"Fellow named Adams left a message for you. He says to find him at the inn." The porter pointed down the street. "Just a few doors down that way. There's a sign hanging out front. You can't miss it."

Revived by this news, Becky smiled and thanked him. Then she renewed her grip on her mother's arm – Gertrude was beginning to look rather faint – and propelled them both down the street toward their final destination. Just a little while longer, she told herself, and the journey would be over at last. There would be a man there who had promised to care for her, someone who could ensure that her mother was cared for as well...

She hadn't realized until just that moment how much faith she was putting in this stranger whom she had never met.

But faith was always rewarded, she told herself, and then they were at the inn.

The sign over the door, swinging in the cold breeze, noted that the establishment was called the Shadow Gulch Inn, with E. Dowser being the proprietor. Inside, the inn was warm and cozy; there was a small entryway with a desk, behind which no one sat but upon which there was a bell to ring for service. Through the first door she could see a neat little sitting room, with a fire blazing cheerfully.

She rang the bell, giving her mother a brave smile, and they waited.

CHAPTER 5

At just about the same time, a young man came down the corridor toward them, and another man poked his head out of the sitting room. The man in the sitting room wore a hat, which he removed at the sight of them, revealing dark brown hair. His eyes were brown, too, she noted, and she was filled with conviction that this was the long-awaited Mr. Walter Adams.

His words left no doubt.

"Miss Vanderhall?"

"Yes, that's me. And you must be Mr. Adams?"

"I am." He waved a hand at her. "Come on in here and sit by the fire. You're cold, I bet."

She did as she was bid, her mother close behind her. Now that she could see all of Mr. Walter Adams, he proved to be a tall, thin man – exactly as advertised – with a receding hairline and the faint beginnings of a black mustache, as though the abdication of his hairline had happened only recently, and he was trying to make up for it. He was watching her closely, and she caught the beginnings of a smile as she came in and sat down near the fire across from him – but she could not help but notice that the smile died quickly as her mother sat beside her.

"And who might this be?"

"This is my mother, Gertrude Vanderhall."

Mr. Adams leaned back in his chair, studying her coolly. "I see. To be clear, you are the girl that the agency sent, are you not?"

"I am," she said. "I applied with them two weeks ago and was matched with you almost immediately. I am glad to know that they told you I was coming."

"I wasn't sure when you would arrive. This is the third day I've spent a few hours here waiting for the coach to show up." His tone was gently jibing, as though the unreliability of cross-country travel was a personal failing on her part. "The agency didn't say anything about you traveling with a posse."

She frowned and opened her mouth to speak, but there was a gentle knock from the door to the sitting room. The three of them turned, and she saw the young man whom she had briefly glimpsed in the hallway. He was rather slight, with ginger-colored hair, and he had a good-natured face that spoke of lots of laughter and good humor. He was smiling, and his smile did not fade at the sight of either her or her mother.

"Good evening, ladies," he said. "Mr. Adams, would you like some tea brought to you here? Martha said she's willing."

Mr. Adams seemed to deliberate for a moment. Then he said, "No, Ethan, I don't think that's necessary. I won't be staying long."

The young man nodded thoughtfully. "Right you are, Mr. Adams. Er – I've had a room made up for your visitor, but perhaps I should have two?"

"No," said Walter Adams. "They're family, they don't mind staying in one room. Besides, at the rates you're charging these days, Ethan, I can't afford to just be paying for rooms for whoever decides to come along on a whim." He turned to Becky. "You'll be staying here until the wedding. Your mother may remain with you, for the time being."

Becky saw her mother flinch at his tone, and she could understand why. Walter Adams was certainly not endearing himself to either of them.

But Ethan only nodded. She got the feeling that he was quite used to the ways of Walter Adams; perhaps that was only natural, if the man had spent the better part of the last three days there in the inn.

"Just as you say, Mr. Adams." He gave a deep, respectful nod to Becky and her mother. "Just let me know if there's anything I can help you with."

Then he was gone, and they were back to Walter alone, who was frowning thoughtfully. He shook his head as though concluding some internal debate, and stood, gesturing to Becky.

"I must get back to my ranch," he said. "Come to the door with me, Miss Vanderhall, if you please."

She touched her mother on the shoulder lightly, to reassure her, and left her there at the fire, following Mr. Adams back out the front door. In the short time that their truncated visit had taken, night had fallen, though it could not be more than four o'clock. She wrapped her arms about herself and shivered, but he didn't seem to notice.

"Again I'll say it, though I hate to repeat myself. There was no mention, no warning, of your mother coming along with you."

"I hardly think that a warning needs to be given," she said, taken aback. "But you're right – the agency didn't know. It… it wasn't settled until just before I left."

"Well, I wish that you would have cleared it with me first."

"I'm sorry, Mr. Adams, but I don't understand the problem."

"She can't live with us," he said shortly. Taken by surprise, she blushed heavily. "I don't mind caring for a wife – I've done it before. But I simply will not have poor relations dragged in on your coattails."

Hot, angry words rushed to Becky's mouth, but she bit them back with difficulty.

With deliberation and care, she said, "I think you've got hold of the wrong end of the stick, Mr. Adams. My mother is certainly not a poor relation. But she is the closest person to me in the world, and I simply could not leave her behind at – in the current situation she was in. I apologize for not telling you in advance, but I did not think it would be so objectionable for your wife to be to have family with her."

"I think you'll find that it's not how Mail Order Brides typically arrive," he said. She could tell that he, too, was trying to control himself; his nostrils were flaring like those of a frightened horse.

"As far as living arrangements, if you object to it, then of course she and I will find another place for her to stay," she said. "She has an income of her own and won't need charity." She knew that her voice was sounding more and more sharp, and that if she didn't halt the interview soon, it would end badly. Getting control of herself once more, she made a final effort. "But we can discuss this at another time. I'm very tired after the journey – and I'm glad to have met you at last. May we speak of our plans tomorrow?"

He narrowed his eyes at her, opened his mouth, shut it again…finally he seemed to reach a decision and nodded, putting his hat back on his head.

"Tomorrow," he said. "I'll be here at one o'clock. Be waiting."

"Certainly, Mr. Adams."

"Good night, Miss Vanderhall." He paused, looking at her keenly. "I must say, the agency got one thing right. You're a beautiful woman."

Then he was gone into the dark street, leaving her standing there for a moment, dumbfounded – and confused at her own reaction. Why did she feel as though he had taken such a liberty, as though he'd shown her unwanted attention? They were engaged to be married, after all. If anyone had a right to comment on her appearance, it was her husband-to-be.

Still, there was a coldness, an impersonal tone to his voice that made her feel a chill down her spine.

She took a moment to collect herself, then slipped back inside to the blessed warmth of the inn.

Her mother, she was gratified to see, was no longer looking as though she wanted to cower in the corner. This was largely, she suspected, down to the fact that the young man,

Ethan, had returned, bearing with him a tea tray. He was in the act of pouring Gertrude a cup, seated across from her in Mr. Adams' vacated chair, chatting away with an easy, genuine friendliness.

"And so, you've only just arrived all the way from Boston? Good gosh, Mrs. Vanderhall, that's quite the undertaking."

"Yes, well, you see, my daughter…" She trailed off as Becky came back in. She turned to her with one of the warmest smiles Becky had seen from her in quite some time. "Becky, did you realize that the nice young man we were speaking to was actually the owner of this establishment?"

"Really?" Becky sat down in her chair again. She felt a wave of exhaustion wash over her. "How kind of you to see to us yourself, Mister—"

"Dowser," he supplied. "According to the sign outside, I'm E. Dowser. But I hope you'll call me Ethan. I like to make friends with my guests whenever I can – that's what keeps them coming back."

He gave her a swift wink, which made her sit up a little straighter in her chair. Ethan Dowser wasn't the most handsome man she'd ever seen, but he had a charm of manner which made it seem so. His eyes were wide and gray and ringed with thick black lashes, as beautiful as a girl's.

He went on, "I thought after I left you three, Ethan, you chump, you should have asked the ladies directly whether they wanted some tea, instead of letting Walter answer for all of them. So I had Martha make up a tray right away. Lo and behold, you and Walter were gone when I got back – but I've been making friends with your mother, anyhow, and a braver and sweeter woman I could never hope to meet." He grinned at Gertrude. "Don't tell me, you're the one who set up your daughter here to marry a man in the West, just so you could have an excuse to go on an adventure."

"Well, not exactly," said Gertrude, blushing furiously and laughing despite herself. Becky couldn't help but chuckle, too.

"It's a story that may take some time in the telling," she said. "But it seems we're going to be availing ourselves of your hospitality, Mr. Dowser, so perhaps we'll get the chance."

He handed her a cup of tea and waved at the plate of biscuits that had come along with it.

"Call me Ethan, please," he said, "because I plan on calling you Gertrude, if you allow it, and I don't want you to feel awkward when you're there being formal all by your lonesome."

She smiled at him.

Becky spoke up. "Well, if it's informality you want, you might call me Becky. Everyone does – except my father. And my mother, when she's feeling stern." She caught a sideways glance from Gertrude and laughed. Ethan chuckled into his cup.

"All right, I accept your challenge. Now, I'll leave you two to recover from your journey. It's about an hour until suppertime. I've taken your bag up to your room – number twelve, incidentally – and I hope you don't mind bunking together after all. If it gets too close in there, let me know and I'll find a spare room for one of you, and we'll just let mum be the word when Walter Adams comes around."

He stood, giving her another wink, and nodded respectfully at Gertrude. "When you're ready for food, come on back to the dining hall, straight down the corridor, you can't miss it. Feel free to wander anywhere in the inn, I have no secrets to hide from my friends. Enjoy yourselves, ladies – after your journey, you deserve it."

He left the room, with the Vanderhall women basking in the glow of his warm personality. For the first time since she had decided to take the plunge and put her plan into action, Becky felt relaxed; and she could tell that her mother was feeling a bit better about things. It was a wonder what a little kindness could do for your soul.

She knew, at the back of her mind, that she shouldn't be wishing that she was engaged to someone like Ethan Dowser rather than Walter Adams.

But she couldn't help wishing it all the same.

CHAPTER 6

For the first time since before she could remember, Becky slept peacefully through the night. She awoke the next morning to a cold, bright early morning sun. Her mother, too, seemed to have let the exhaustion of the last few weeks catch up with her, and was still slumbering on the other side of the bed.

Becky rose and washed at the basin in the corner of the room. The water was icy cold, but it felt refreshing. She dressed quickly and stepped to the window, looking out over the street.

In the morning, Shadow Gulch was just as quaint and provincial as it had seemed the night before, but she saw now how the dim afternoon light had softened the hard edges of the town. It was a rough place, to be sure, with uneven wooden walkways, rutted dirt roads, and clapboard sidings on all the buildings. She felt doubly grateful for her current position inside the cozy little inn.

On that thought, she decided it was time to go and explore her surroundings.

It was quiet downstairs, but she heard the faint clink of crockery coming from the direction of the dining hall. The clock on the wall told her it was not yet the breakfast hour – she had been informed by Martha, the cook, that she served precisely from eight to nine in the morning, not a moment before, not a moment after – and there was no one in the dining hall. She followed the sounds to the door of the kitchen and was hesitating on the threshold, unsure of whether she should enter, when the door swung open, and Ethan Dowser nearly ran right into her.

They sprang back from each other, and he let out a laugh.

"Talk about walking on little cat feet." he said. "I didn't hear you come to the door."

"I'm sorry," she said, blushing ferociously. "I was just looking around – curiosity got the better of me, I suppose."

"Aw, don't apologize. You're a friend of mine, and friends are welcome to go anywhere in this house. You're up earlier than I thought you would be, after the journey you had. Did you sleep well?"

"Oh, yes, it was – it was delightful, to be honest, to sleep in a real bed after all that time on the train and in the stagecoach and at horrible little waysides. Thank you so much for your hospitality, Mister … I mean, Ethan."

He smiled at her, and she couldn't help but smile back.

"Well, the pleasure is all mine, Miss … I mean, Becky. Will you take a cup of coffee with me? It's a little while yet before breakfast, but I'd appreciate the company."

All she could manage to do was nod, smiling so hard she thought her face might crack.

He was very pleasant company, chatting and smiling and laughing, very solicitous about her story. When he heard her confess that she had run away from an arranged marriage, he shook his head and tsk-tsked.

"It's a terrible thing," he said. "Men are supposed to take care of women, but so many of them don't pay any heed to the privilege and the responsibility. I'm sorry you had to make such a choice, Becky."

"I'm more sorry for my mother than I am for myself," she said. "Poor thing, she still doesn't know what to think. And I'm very sorry to say that Mr. Adams made a very poor showing last night when we met – he didn't speak to Mother at all, and he gave me quite a tongue lashing for daring to bring her with me without asking him first."

"Well, I can't say I'm surprised about that," said Ethan frankly. "Far be it from me to speak badly about Walter Adams without cause, but he's not a very…jolly fellow, I suppose I would say. Taciturn. Not much given to friendly overtures."

"Well, not all men can be like you, Ethan."

He looked slightly taken back by her frankness, and then he grinned at her.

"I'm going to take that as a compliment."

"You ought to," she said softly, fighting a blush. Sensing her discomfort, he pressed on.

"The fact is, Walter's got his own history, and I guess it might explain his actions a little if I tell you. So don't think that I'm spreading gossip – I just want you to have the best chance of understanding. Knowing more might be of help to you. And I ain't sure he'll tell you what happened himself. Well, it's like this. I suppose you know Walter calls himself a widower."

"Yes, it was in his letter of application. His first wife passed away some three years ago, I believe."

"And that's absolutely true, she did. Poor thing died of a fever – she was a sweet young lady."

"You knew her?"

"Sure." He shrugged. "I've run this inn for over a decade now – you might not think it to look at me, but I'll be thirty next month, and I inherited it from my grandfather when I was seventeen. Grew up here in Shadow Gulch, know all the locals. I remember when Walter and Elsie got married – she was hardly more than a kid then. And Walter was much the same as he is now, taciturn and keeping himself to himself, but apparently women don't mind that if the gentleman is a handsome devil – as I've been told Walter is."

Becky laughed. "I suppose so. I can't really say that I noticed that much. I was too busy just trying to get to know him a bit."

"Well, you never get a second chance to make a first impression, so I'm sure Walter will rue his crankiness to the end of his days. I can't tell you exactly what happened between Walter and his young bride, but Elsie's mother came to stay after they had been married about a year – and within two months, Elsie and her mother had left."

Becky sat up straight. "What?"

"Yes." Ethan nodded. "They done ran off, leaving Walter to fend for himself. Walter called himself a widower straight away, but the truth is he was made into a bachelor again against his will. Elsie and her ma went east, and she never came back again. And then, of course, the poor thing died. I may not know what happened, but I know for a fact that Walter blames Elsie's ma for Elsie's decision to run out on him."

"Why on earth…"

Ethan shook his head. "I dunno. And I wouldn't want to speculate, not about something like that – but it doesn't leave a very good taste in your mouth, does it? Certainly, it didn't in Walter's. I reckon that's the cause behind his impoliteness to your poor mother. He's painted all mothers-in-law with the same brush, regardless of whether they deserve it or not."

"They certainly do not all deserve it," said Becky. "My mother believes so firmly in the holiness of the marriage vow that this whole time we were traveling I was worried that she would run back to…" She stopped, and Ethan raised an inquiring eyebrow. "Oh – I suppose I'd better not talk about that."

"No need to say anything if it makes you uncomfortable," Ethan told her. "But like I said, I consider anyone who stays beneath my roof to be a friend. And if a friend needs someone to talk to, well – I'm always here."

Becky hesitated, waffling between keeping silent and letting the truth spill out. Finally, she could not help herself, and the words came rushing through.

She told him about her father, and about why she'd decided that she had to leave. She told him about how afraid she'd been to leave her mother there alone – how afraid she was that her father would find out her plans – that he might somehow hunt her down even now.

Ethan nodded, listening keenly.

When the words finally began to falter and run dry, he reached over and put a hand comfortingly on hers.

"I hope you won't think I'm taking liberties," he said, "but I only want to tell you that I know what it's like. I told you that I inherited this place from my grandfather – well, he was my mother's pa. My poor ma did her best with a husband who was cruel and who beat her, but she finally had to leave when he took to beating me, too. We holed up with my grandfather and spent a happy life here until she died when I was ten."

He was quiet for a moment, and she simply watched him as he sorted through his memories, both painful and sweet. She shifted in her chair with the realization of the sudden and unexpected attachment she felt to this man she had only just met, the feeling that they seemed to share.

When his eyes returned to hers, they were filled with a faint puzzlement, and she knew he saw something on her face that was better hidden away.

With effort, she looked away from his mesmerizing gray eyes, scolding herself for her feelings.

"I-I appreciate your insight into Mr. Adams," she finally stammered. "I'll do my best to remember that he has a history, just as I do."

"I find that it helps to remember that with everyone," Ethan said, regaining his composure. "Very few folks grow up in peace and harmony, these days." He stood. "Well, it's almost eight o'clock. Should you go and wake your mother? I'd hate to have her miss breakfast."

"Yes. Yes, of course. Thank you."

She hesitated for a moment and watched him go back into the kitchen. Then shook her head with a sigh.

"Really, Rebecca," she told herself sternly, "get ahold of yourself. He is not the man you came here to marry."

CHAPTER 7

The man Rebecca came there to marry duly presented himself at one o'clock, just as he had stated the evening before. She decided not to push her mother on him for the time being and met him in the sitting room alone. They had tea together, making small talk that was rather painful and strange, especially after the quick close talk she had so recently enjoyed with Ethan Dowser.

Finally, he stood. "Will you take a turn around the town with me, Miss Vanderhall?" he asked. "I can't just sit here all afternoon. I'm an active man and must at least be walking if I'm not working."

It was cold outside, and the sun had given way to silver-gray snow clouds. Rebecca collected her warm coat and her hat, and followed him outside, feeling a faint sense of déjà vu.

As they walked, she asked him a question or two about ranching. He answered in what seemed to be as few words as possible, and finally said, "If you're so interested in the process, I would be happy to find you a book on the subject."

"I'm sorry," she said, taken aback. "I'm only trying to take an interest in your work – after all, if we're to be married, what matters to you will matter to me."

"I'm sorry," he said gruffly. "Of course."

She lapsed into silence for a few moments, but the silence was just as awkward as the conversation had been.

"Have you always lived here in Shadow Gulch?"

He sighed, seeming to relent from his bad mood. "I was raised in Bellville, about five miles from here. My father bought the ranch here in Shadow Gulch when I was fifteen – I've worked it ever since. My mother passed away when I was small, and Pa died about ten years ago."

"I'm sorry to hear that."

"Don't be," he said. "He was a bitter old cuss. He couldn't walk through Shadow Gulch on a day like this without complaining about everything he saw..." He stopped walking, staring at a few children in their path. "Hey there! You kids. You can't play in the middle of the walkway. There are adults trying to get by."

He hauled Becky to the side along with him past the hapless youths, grumbling under his breath. She gave them an apologetic smile.

By the time he was done walking her around town and, perhaps showing her off to the townspeople of Shadow Gulch, she was relieved to be deposited at the inn once more. They said their good-byes, and Becky gave him a wave as he departed.

Well, all in all, it hadn't been a total disaster. And she had made some progress in getting to know him. Perhaps in time, when he realized she wouldn't run away with her mother, some of his harshness would fade. Surely, there was a kinder man hiding inside his bluster.

It was getting on for evening time, just an hour or two shy of what they called suppertime, and she stepped into the inn to discover the most delicious smell of baking bread. She followed her nose into the dining room and stopped in the doorway, smiling at the picture that was presented to her there.

Ethan and a few young boys were in the process of putting up garlands of greenery for the holiday all around the walls, lending the dining hall quite a festive air. Her mother, Becky was delighted to see, was seated in the corner giving them directions.

"No, to the right a little, I think, Ethan. No, my right. That's right."

"Right, is it?" Ethan called over his shoulder with a grin.

"I mean to say…that is correct." Gertrude laughed, and Becky blinked in surprise. When was the last time she had heard her mother laugh like that, completely free of any nervousness or constraint, not simply laughing because it was expected of her?

She couldn't remember, and for a moment, the sadness of that caught at her. But there was too much jolliness going on in the dining hall for her to sink into despair with her memories, and she made the decision to cast off the sadness and join in the fun.

"I think you should just start all over again," she called out, stepping into the room. "After all, I'm here now, and my standards are much stricter than my mother's."

Ethan laughed, coming down from the ladder. The boys continued to put up the garlands, and he came to join Becky and Gertrude at the small round table in the corner.

"Did you have a pleasant walk?" he inquired.

Becky rubbed at her eyes with her fingertips. "I enjoyed the walk," she said.

"Oh, good," murmured Gertrude, smiling, but Ethan eyed her keenly. There was a call from the kitchen for Gertrude to come and try out the stuffing that Martha was making for Christmas dinner, and Ethan took the opportunity to lean forward on the table and ask Becky further about the day.

"I'm glad you had a good walk. I was a bit worried. You feeling better about things?"

She shook her head, suddenly feeling rather miserable. "I s'pose," she said, not wanting to reveal too much.

"Well, don't be too discouraged. I'm sure it will all work out," Ethan said sympathetically. "Like I said, sometimes Walter comes across a bit harsh."

"I-I…" She paused and then continued, "Thank you, Ethan. I… Well, I want to make sure I'm not making a mistake. I have my mother to think about, too. I feel very responsible for her."

"You may not have to marry him," Ethan said, lowering his eyes to the table. "As I understand it, arrangements such as the one through the matrimonial agency are not like regular engagements – it isn't as though he can … sue you for breach of contract."

His comment made her laugh, despite how she felt. "I suppose not," she said. "But I did make a commitment, Ethan – and I can't back out simply because I'm having second thoughts about it now."

"No?" he asked softly.

She shook her head, determinedly. "No. I've seen my father back out of commitments far too often. He would make a business arrangement, and then perhaps find something that suited him better or something that would work to his advantage some other way and break his promises without a second thought. Whatever I do, I can't behave like my father would. I just *can't.* Sometimes, I ask myself what he would do, and then I do the opposite."

Ethan was smiling again, his moment of soft questioning gone, and when he met her gaze his gray eyes were alight.

"I suppose that's one way to navigate through life."

"It's the only way I know."

"Well, it led you here, so I won't quibble with it."

They sat for a moment in the warmth of the room, which smelled like pine and Christmas, and simply smiled at each other.

Not for the first time, Becky wondered how she had managed to make such a quick, close connection to Ethan, when even simple communication with the man she was engaged to marry seemed beyond her grasp entirely.

CHAPTER 8

The next few days went by swiftly, though they followed much the same pattern as the first day after their arrival. Becky rose early and spent the first hour of her day sitting with Ethan, chatting over coffee. He continued to be a pleasant companion, asking her questions about her childhood and her favorite things, her hopes and plans for the future, and even questioning seriously about what her mother might like for a Christmas present.

When he asked the first time, Becky laughed.

"I don't think you need to get us Christmas presents," she said. "We're only guests at your inn, not long-lost family members come to visit."

"Nonsense," Ethan said, waving a careless hand. "You're friends, just as I've told you before, and if I can do something to make you happy, you'd better believe that I will. Now, if you can't think of anything your mother would like or use, I'll be forced to get her something entirely frivolous, like a box of chocolates from back east where you came from."

"Oh, dear," Becky told him, wrinkling her nose. "I'm afraid you just don't understand women."

"Oh, no?"

"No. Ethan, chocolate is never frivolous."

Spending regular time alone with him put a charge on her day and brightened the skies outside no matter what the weather. It also, she was aware, made it ever more difficult to spend time with Walter Adams – for her betrothed certainly suffered in the comparison.

But she was no less determined to make things work between her and Walter now than she had been when she first arrived, and each time she felt her heart sink as the one o'clock hour drew near, she told herself sternly, "Rebecca, you really must learn to control yourself."

Walter arrived punctually at one o'clock each afternoon, sat for tea with her in the sitting room, and then took her for a turn about town. He never spoke about setting a date for their wedding, and she held off questioning him about it, since he seemed rather sensitive to her questioning him about anything at all.

She was always very punctual herself, as it was evident that he appreciated this quality. It was only after she had been there for just less than a week that she got rather caught up in what she was doing and completely forgot about the time.

It was after their usual lunch time – only they called lunch "dinner" here in the west, which confused her for a while – and Ethan had shared a new idea for the decorations in the dining hall. He'd explained it to them with such excitement and enthusiasm that Gertrude had clapped her hands and asked whether they couldn't make the alterations then and there.

It was only Becky who had an objection.

"But – mistletoe?" she said. "Isn't that rather, well…likely to lead to… awkward… incidents?"

Ethan laughed.

"The incidents couldn't be any more awkward than that sentence," he said. "Are you worried someone's going to kiss you and you won't be ready for it, Miss Rebecca?"

He winked at her, and she blushed hotly, knowing it could theoretically happen, and she would be unable to do anything to stop it. She had a feeling that he, too, knew she was going to blush at his suggestion, and had made it on purpose to achieve exactly that desired result.

"Well, if no one else is worried about it, then I'm not, either," she declared. "I don't suppose you know where to find mistletoe around here."

"As a matter of fact," Ethan told her, grinning, "a friend of mine brought in several bunches of it this very morning. I only waited until dinner to suggest it because I could use the extra help putting it up."

And extra help was exactly what he got. After that conversation, Becky didn't feel she could very well bow out of the work. With Gertrude bustling about making little wreaths and bundles of the mistletoe, Ethan got out the step ladder and enlisted Becky's help in hanging the greenery from different parts of the room.

As she tied it above the kitchen door, he held firmly onto the sides of the stepladder. She looked down at him and laughed.

"Are you so worried that the door will fling open suddenly?"

"It could happen," he said. "Far be it from me to be the cause of someone getting a broken bone."

"Oh, I'm sure I'd land on something soft. You're right underneath me, after all."

He grinned up at her. "Maybe so…"

She quickly turned her attention back to her work tying the knot, shaking her head and trying not to blush with shame. She should never have said such a thing.

"There." She came down a step and stopped, as his arms were in the way. Now she was only a foot above him. "What do you think of that?"

"Not bad," Ethan said. "But how do you know it will work?"

"Work?" She raised her eyebrows but found when she looked at him that he was staring up at her very intently. She shivered, knowing she was in dangerous territory.

His gaze didn't waver.

She had no idea what to say next when there came the sound of a harrumph from the far door: someone clearing his throat very deliberately to announce their presence.

"Oh, Mr. Adams."

Ethan dropped his arms immediately, and Becky stepped down on the ground safely once more, smoothing her dress and trying to put her hair back in place from where it had escaped its bonds.

"I didn't see you there," she continued, feeling like a wayward schoolgirl.

"I waited for ten minutes," said Walter reproachfully, "and then I thought I'd better come investigate and see what was keeping you." He eyed Ethan. "Or who."

Becky coughed. "I-I'm so sorry, Mr. Adams. I'll just – I'll just fetch my coat."

"Don't you want tea? We always have tea," he responded.

"Can't we simply go for a walk today, just this once?" she pleaded with him. She was suddenly desperate to get out of the house, and perhaps the cool air of the outside would take care of the hot blush that she felt flaming her cheeks. "It's a beautiful day, and I've already taken up so much of your time."

He hesitated, and she was positive he was going to reject her proposal, though she was equally positive that he didn't enjoy the teatime in the sitting room any more than she did. But then he nodded, and she saw him dart another swift glance at Ethan, who had already turned solicitously to Gertrude to get her opinion on the new decorations.

It was that day, as they walked through the empty town, that he said, "I've been thinking about the most appropriate time for our wedding ceremony, and I've decided that we shall be married the day before Christmas Eve."

She gawped at him.

"S-so soon?" she stammered, even though there was really no reason to delay further. Yet, it was only a few days left until Christmas.

"It makes the most sense to have it over and done with before the holiday," he said. "People are busy with their families during Christmas, and I want to stay at home for at least a few days afterward."

"Oh...I had hoped that I could spend the holiday with my mother," she ventured becoming very worried indeed about her mother. "I don't suppose you'd mind her coming out to stay, just for the day or two..."

"I'm surprised you'd ask, after everything we've discussed."

It was as clear a rejection as could be stated without actually saying the word no. Becky felt her heart sink.

He walked even more swiftly and efficiently than usual that day, almost as though he were making some sort of a point. Not much later, he deposited her back at the inn without more conversation. As she steeled herself to say goodbye to him in something at least approaching a fond manner, he stopped and looked at her keenly.

"You should come out to the ranch house," he said abruptly.

She blinked. "I beg your pardon?"

"Tomorrow," he told her. "When I come to collect you for our outing, I will bring the horse and buggy, and I'll take you out to the ranch. I suppose you'd like to at least see where you're going to be living for the rest of your life."

She wished he hadn't used such terminal phrasing.

"Er – yes," she said. "You're quite right. I'd very much like to see the ranch. Thank you, Walter."

There was a pause, and she realized suddenly that it was the first time that she had addressed him by his first name. She froze. How would he react? Would he think she was being impolite? Taking liberties?

It occurred to her that it was a strange thing to worry about. After all, within a week's time, she would be married to the man. And here she was scaring herself with what-ifs simply because she had used his first name.

Why, she'd been using Ethan's first name not five minutes after they met.

But, to her relief, her slip of the tongue did not appear to have made Walter angry. He was tense for a moment, but then his face actually relaxed.

However, all he said in reply was, "You are quite welcome, Miss Vanderhall."

He tipped his hat, and went on his way, leaving her to enter the inn by herself. She did, grateful as ever for the warmth inside, and wondering when she had come to consider being called "Miss Vanderhall" an insult.

CHAPTER 9

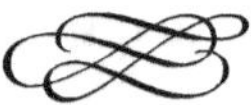

Ethan said, "So that's your Christmas present to us all, is it? Getting married?"

She had waited until the next morning to tell him that the date was set. She was not at her best that morning; for the first time since she had arrived at the Shadow Gulch Inn, proprietor E. Dowser, she had not slept well at all. At one point during the night, her mother had even reached over and touched her shoulder timidly to ask her if she was quite all right, and that was when Becky realized how much she was tossing and turning.

But now it was morning time – coffee and chat time with Ethan – and the realization washed over her very suddenly, how much she would miss this when she was gone.

It was a gray day, reflecting her mood, and she had decided to embrace it, wearing her dark gray dress.

"I don't know why you should consider it a Christmas present," she said slowly, trying to determine what his tone was meant to convey. She sought out his gaze, but he was looking solemnly into his cup of coffee as though the meaning of life were hidden there amidst the cloud of cream. "I suppose it's better to have things settled, get ready to move on – this was only a way station, after all."

He did look up at that, and she knew she was not imagining the spark of hurt in his gray eyes. But he masked it glibly after only a second, and said, "What will your mother do?"

"I-I haven't told her yet. And I had so hoped that we could be together for the holiday. I had hoped to pave the way for her…" She twined her fingers together anxiously. Gently, he reached out and put a hand on hers.

"You take after your mother at all times," he said, "but when I see you get anxious like this, that's when you look the most like her. Listen, Becky – I don't want to stick my oar in where it's not wanted, but – are you quite sure you want to marry Walter Adams? Whenever you go out for a walk with him you come back looking as though he kicked every puppy you came across."

She pulled her hands from his touch and took a deep breath.

"It isn't really a question of what I want," she said, "not anymore. It's a question of what I promised to do. I made an arrangement in order to escape from my father, and I can't go back on that now. I owe Walter."

"You owe yourself more," Ethan said gently. "Don't tie yourself to a life you don't want simply out of a sense of obligation. How would that be any different from the life you ran away from?"

His words were simple and true – and they stung all the more because of it. She put her hands in her lap, sitting up straight.

"Obviously we don't look at things the same way," she said, hating how stiff her voice sounded. "I can't turn my back on an obligation just because of…how I feel."

"Feelings are the best reason to change your obligations, I would say."

"I'm sorry, Ethan, but – I can't go by your opinion in this matter. It's my decision, and it was made long before we met – I mean before we came here."

His eyes caught hers and rested on them for a moment, and she saw the spark of something true and bright churn in their depths. Then he nodded and stood up from the table.

"Well, if you're going to see the ranch, this is a good time to do it," he said. "It's as dismal and dark outside as could be.

The ranch will at least look bright and welcoming by comparison."

Evidently, he had no more to say on the subject, for he disappeared for the rest of the morning and did not come in for lunch. As one o'clock neared, Becky fidgeted, trying not to look obvious that she was looking for Ethan – and looking in vain.

Her mother noticed, of course, but in true Gertrude style, chose not to say anything about it. Instead, she just put a hand on her daughter's shoulder and squeezed comfortingly, smiling at her.

"Martha has told me that the next step is to make up the dough for the cinnamon bread. She says that they make it every year, and it must rise for a good while. We'll do a batch of it this evening for practice, and then finish it the day before Christmas Eve. Will you help us, Becky?"

Becky couldn't help but flinch at her reference to the day before Christmas Eve – her wedding day. She still had not been able to bring herself to tell her mother what Walter had proposed.

"Yes – yes, of course, Mother. But you know I'll be a bit later getting back this evening, since Walter is taking me to see the ranch."

"Oh, right." Gertrude wilted a little. "I wish I could see the place where you're going to live…"

Becky took her hand and squeezed it, trying to return the comfort.

"I wish you could, too," she said. "And maybe – maybe I can convince him. I haven't given up. I brought you with me here so that we could be together."

She had hoped for a stout, "Right." from her mother, but all she received was another smile, a wan one this time, but then she spoke, "I've left my husband to come here, Becky, and I have to admit it's changed my way of thinking—being here and away from… Well, away from *him*. But you… I want you to be very sure of things. Very sure. Otherwise, it is likely you'll find yourself in the same position as I…"

With that for her encouragement, Becky went out to meet Walter outside at one o'clock.

He was there on the dot, of course, neither early nor late, and as she stepped outside the front door of the inn, he was pulling up to the wooden sidewalk with the horse and buggy. He touched his hat and nodded to her, but he made no motion to get down and help her into the buggy. She crossed around to the other side, uncomfortably aware that they were being stared at by all the passers-by; he seemed to relish the attention and nodded gravely to everyone he made eye contact with.

"Good morning, Walter," she said.

"Good afternoon," he corrected her, and whistled to the horse.

The ranch that had belonged to Walter's father, "And which will one day be passed on to our son," was about a ten-minute drive outside of Shadow Gulch—as long as the horse was going at a brisk trot – which he was, since Walter continually laid on with the whip if he showed any sign of slowing, even when pulling up a hill. The fields were muddy and half-covered with snow, and Becky thought they were distinctly unprepossessing. Perhaps another layer of snow would return the magical touch to the countryside, she thought, the touch she had noticed over a week before, when she and her mother had pulled through on this road in the stagecoach.

It seemed a lifetime ago. Things had changed so much – Shadow Gulch had been both more and less than she expected, somehow.

But whatever happened, her life would never be the same.

The ranch house itself was small and neat, but she understood Ethan's comment about it. It did seem to be rather gloomy, standing alone on a stretch of bare ground as though it had been ostracized by every other creature and thing. She got herself down to the ground and followed Walter up the steps to the veranda, which was bare of chairs and benches. He opened the door and she noted that the hall was just as bare, apart from the rifle that was hung on the wall just inside.

"This is a lovely porch," she offered, searching for something to say that wouldn't stir up his sourness. "You must enjoy sitting out here in the summer evenings, watching the sun go down."

"I never sit out here in the summer, evenings or not," he said. "I have far too much work to do to sit around. I hope you don't labor under the misconception that this is going to be an easy life, Miss Vanderhall, being the wife of a rancher. There's always something to do, something that must be done so things don't simply fall apart."

"Of course, I don't expect a life of ease," she said readily. "And I don't mind hard work. I was raised to set my hand to whatever task needed to be done – why, even while we've been at the inn, my mother and I have been helping to decorate for Christmas."

He paused just inside the door and turned a keen eye on her.

"Hmm," he said. "Yes. I noticed. Well, there will be much more to do here than simply a few decorations for a holiday, mark my words. This is a working ranch, and I like my house to be kept clean and neat, my suppers regular, my floors swept. That ought to keep you occupied, and if it doesn't, I can always use someone to help bring in the cows in the evening."

She smiled. "I don't think I'd mind that," she said. "Helping the cows come home."

He sniffed, but she could tell he did not approve of her little joke. Meekly, she followed him through the house toward the kitchen. There was no fire in the fireplace, but a few glowing embers; he stirred them up and nodded toward the kettle on the stove.

"The pump is just outside. Make us some tea, will you?"

"I'd be happy to, Walter."

She was grateful to walk away for a few moments and have a moment to gather herself. Even the creaking and balkiness of the pump did not faze her; she took as much time as she dared, and then carried the bucket back inside, steeling herself for the next step.

"I think the house is lovely," she told him as she poured water into the kettle and set it on the arm over the fire, which was now roaring. "And you say that your father built it?"

"He did."

"It's amazing. Quite a feat."

He squinted at her suspiciously. "Why do you say that?"

She had no reason why. She wasn't even entirely certain what she was saying anymore.

"It's, well, it's quite a spacious house," she rushed on, before he could demand a reason for her words once more. "How many rooms are there?"

"A sitting room, a parlor, a dining room downstairs," he said. "And three bedrooms upstairs."

"Three bedrooms. Ah, there's plenty of room."

He looked up at her as she brought him a cup for his tea, his eyes narrowed again. It was extremely uncomfortable, trying to pick and choose her words in a way that wouldn't set him off – but it appeared that she had managed to do so again, however inadvertently.

"Plenty of room for what?"

"Well – for children, of course," she said, and then, because her mouth was speaking faster than her brain could force it to keep still, "and if Mother came to visit once in a while, why, she wouldn't put us out at all. And she's a hard worker too," she assured him. "That's where I get it from, you see. She would come and help, and she wouldn't be a nuisance or get in the way at all."

"I thought," he said, pushing his cup away, "that I made myself clear on that issue – very clear indeed. Your mother will not come and stay with us, and that's final."

She sat down next to him and reached for his hand, but he pulled it away.

"Walter," she said beseechingly, "I think it's time that we talked about this. I know you have a past – and I have one, too. I haven't even told you, but the truth is I ran away from my father. That's why my mother is here with me – because my father is a cruel man, and I couldn't bear to leave her there to face him alone."

His face was frozen, and getting stonier by the moment, but she plunged haphazardly on. She couldn't stop now.

"But I know you have your own sad story from your past – I know what your wife did, and that you blame her mother for it. I cannot hope to make it up to you for what's been done, but I can promise you that it won't be like that – it would never be like that with my mother and me. I promise you, Walter."

She paused at last, her eyes searching his, but there was no spark of warmth in his brown eyes, and he met her gaze almost robotically.

Voice low, he said, "Who told you about that?"

"Why, I heard it from…er…"

Suddenly she realized, in the face of his anger, that she had made a serious error in judgement.

"You heard it from that little inn keeper, didn't you?" he said, his tone turning even angrier. He stood up slowly, and placed his hands on the table, pressing down as though trying to keep them from getting loose. "I knew it. I knew when I saw you two together that you were getting close – too close."

"No, Walter, it isn't like that…"

"And then he goes and fills your mind with poisonous lies about me – lies about how my wife left me – lies about how she fled…"

Still seated, she looked up at him, and felt the first twinges of fear. How could he claim that it was a lie? How could he say his wife hadn't left when it was easily proven?

But she understood. His pride wouldn't let him admit it. And if he did admit it, he had to blame it on someone else – on his first wife's poor mother. He couldn't bear to accept the guilt nor the blame as his own.

And she knew now that it must have been his own actions that caused it. If he was cruel now, he likely had been cruel then. One hand lifted as though he could no longer control it, and drew back – he was poised to hit her, to strike her across the face, and she knew for a certainty that his wife had fled, with the help of her loving mother, to start over again somewhere new…

Knew it for a certainty because she had already done that exact thing.

Suddenly it wasn't Walter Adams standing in front of her but her father. She blinked hard, willing the hazy vision to disappear, and it did, drifting into smoke, revealing the hard, furious face of her husband-to-be.

She found herself wondering how any girl, however desperate, could ever have found him handsome.

With an effort that was obvious, he lowered his hand to the table once more, where he pressed it down flat, trembling. When he spoke next, his voice was low and dangerous.

"Do you know what? I feel as though the only right thing to do is to write to the matrimonial agency and demand my money back."

Shaking, she pushed to a stand.

"I think you're right," she said stiffly. "I think both of us are better off pretending that our engagement never happened."

He shook his head. "You misunderstand me, Miss Vanderhall," he said. "I intend to get my money back from the matrimonial agency – but I intend to get my money's worth from you. I've said that I'll marry you on the day before Christmas Eve, and I'll be cursed if anything is going to stop me from doing so."

She took a step back. "You can't be serious. After all this?"

"I am serious – deadly serious. I've already shown you off to the town, told them to expect the wedding. I've endured enough sympathy and pity from them over the last five years – I won't let it happen again."

"I intended to keep my promise to you this whole time," she said, and she could hear her voice shaking. "But after your display of temper this afternoon, I know enough to walk away – I value myself enough to put an end to our engagement before it's too late."

The twist of his lip, the jeer which he directed to her, the anger just beneath it, was almost terrifying. Again, she thought of her father, and wondered if her mother had gone through this exact same thing before they were married, or if he had saved the awful truth for afterward.

Walter Adams had stepped forward and caught her by the wrist, and however hard she twisted, she could not get loose.

"I don't think so," he said. "I'm not a man who backs away from his commitments – and I won't let you do it, either. We promised to marry each other, Rebecca Vanderhall, and that's what we're going to do, if I have to keep you locked up until the wedding day."

How she made it up the stairs, she couldn't recall. She knew she had resisted as much as she could, and perhaps he'd had to carry her – but the next thing she knew, she found herself in a locked bedroom.

It was obviously not his bedroom, for which she was grateful. Instead, it was small and appointed with a few feminine touches that made her suspect that either Walter's first wife had used it as a sewing room, or her mother had spent her few months visiting in this very room.

Becky crawled to the window and looked out. The house was tall, and she was on the second story. There were no trees she could try to climb down. To leap down from this height meant the risk of twisting or even breaking her ankle. She tried the windows nonetheless and found that they could not be opened more than a few inches. There were nails on the outside keeping them from opening fully.

She had heard him lock the door. She was well and truly trapped.

Already it was growing dark. Despairing, she sat by the window and watched the light fade from the sky. There was no moonlight, but as she watched, she became aware of a faint glow. It puzzled her at first, and then she realized the glow was coming from the snow that had begun to fall.

It was almost eerie, but strangely comforting at the same time, to watch the storm settle over the house like a blanket. She wondered how it was that snow could cast such a light, even without anything to reflect from – and then wondered how horrible men like her father and Walter Adams could exist in the same world that provided her with such beautiful miracles.

One thing was for certain – no matter what, she would not marry him. He could not force her, after all. He had nothing to hold over her head…

Except, perhaps, her mother.

The thought of it made her blood run cold. Suppose he went back into town in the morning and told her mother that she was invited to come and stay at the house after all? Suppose he threatened to harm her if her daughter didn't marry him?

Oh, Becky could only hope the thought wouldn't occur to him.

But there was nothing to be done about it. She couldn't warn Gertrude – she couldn't even tell her she was safe, for the time being. She could only sit by the window, curled in a ball, and try to trust that everything would be all right, somehow.

Perhaps when the morning came, things would be different.

She'd been in a position like this before, after all. Perhaps her marriage to Reginald Rogers hadn't been quite so imminent, but it had certainly loomed over her much like this occasion did. She had only two days before Walter Adams intended to marry her – two days to plan her escape.

Planning was a better use of her time than crying, but Becky did both.

She had just about worn herself out with plotting different potential avenues of escape and wiping tears from her eyes simultaneously when she heard a strange sound from afar off, through the two inches of open window.

She pressed closer to the window, squinting into the darkness, trying to see.

What was that noise? It was a strange one, a muffled thump-thump, like a far off heartbeat…

Or like a horse riding down a road that was covered by snow.

She sat up straight, elation darting through her with a powerful force. It was quite clear to her that Walter Adams didn't have any friends, certainly none that would come calling on him this late in the evening. No, the only person it could possibly be…

…was E. Dowser, Proprietor of the Shadow Gulch Inn.

As much as the snow was glowing with its ethereal light, she could not see the shape of the horse as it drew closer. She did hear the shout of challenge that came from outside, however, and her heart leapt. Yes, though she couldn't see his form, she would recognize that voice anywhere.

"Walter Adams. Bring her out."

There was nothing but silence, and she wondered whether Walter had indeed left the house. Perhaps, she thought bitterly, he was helping the cows to come home.

"If you don't bring her out, Mr. Adams, I'm going to be forced to come in and get her."

Finally, she heard the laconic voice of her intended, calling out to Ethan.

"What right do you have, Mr. Dowser, to set foot on private property?"

"You've kidnapped a woman, Walter. That's enough right for any red-blooded man to step in."

"I've kidnapped no one. You saw for yourself that she set foot in my buggy of her own free will – that's right, I saw you spying from behind the window." Walter laughed, a long, ugly, slow chuckle like molasses in the wintertime. "I don't know what game you think you're playing, Ethan, but you've already lost. The girl said she would marry me come the day before Christmas Eve, and that's precisely what's going to happen."

"She may have gotten into your buggy of her own free will, but I'm darn sure she's not still in your house for the same reason," shouted Ethan. The righteous anger in his voice made her feel a glow down to her fingertips. "You've lured her here under false pretenses, if nothing else. She planned to be back this evening to help her mother with the Christmas bread. Her poor ma is half out of her mind with worry and asked me to come and collect her. I'd say her ma has more of a right to her presence tonight than you do, given that you're *not* married. And if you're thinking you can convince her to do what you want, whatever dastardly plan you have in mind – well, I'd bet on Becky a million times over before I'd give a penny for your chances."

"Is that a fact?"

She could picture Ethan's handsome face, rigid with determination.

"That's a fact," he said tersely.

She heard the front door creak open further and knew Walter was going out to meet him. They would have a fight there in the front yard, in the dark, in the snow – but Walter, she realized with a dart of fear, was almost certain to be armed. She had seen the rifle he kept inside the door, and she would not put it past him to use it on Ethan, though of course the innkeeper would likely not be armed himself. And then Walter would claim that Ethan was trespassing, and when she protested, he would claim she didn't know what she was talking about.

She could see it all happening as clearly as though history were laid out in front of her.

She *had to do something.*

The window wasn't going to give. She rushed across the room to the door and pushed on it again. Yes, it was locked, she'd already tried it numerous times. But she hadn't stormed it over and over, knowing the noise would bring Walter. But what did that matter now? Besides, Walter was occupied outside.

She hesitated for only a moment, searching the room around her. In the gloom, she located the chair that was pushed up against the wall and picked it up. It was reassuringly solid in her hands.

She faced the door again.

"It's you or me, door," she said.

Breathing a silent, quick prayer, she rushed at it, holding the chair before her. The bang of the impact made her recoil, but she recovered quickly and tried again.

From behind her, drifting in the window, she heard Walter cry, "What in tarnation…"

Twice, three times, and once more, and she could feel the door giving way under her assault. She was short of breath, but she continued on, so anxious to be out that she would have clawed her way through the door if the chair hadn't been faster.

By the time she made the first splinter through the panel, she could hear the front door slam.

By the time the chair leg made it through completely, she heard footsteps thundering up the stairs.

By the time the space was almost wide enough to put the entire chair through, there was a key fumbling at the lock. In the gloom of the corridor, she could see Walter staring at her wide-eyed, as taken aback at her actions as she might herself have been if she had slowed down enough to think of them. She stood still for a second, staring at him, and then threw the chair at him.

He shoved it aside, of course, still staring. She saw a shadow creeping up the stairs behind him.

"What the tarnation are you doing?"

Becky was still panting and out of breath, but she managed to reply, "Breaking free."

The shadow leapt forward, and when Walter felt the muzzle of his own rifle pressed against his back, he stepped back very deliberately, raising his hands—an expression of fury and defeat mingled on his face.

"I told you," said Ethan, sounding more like himself now, his voice full of hidden laughter. "Always, always bet on Becky."

CHAPTER 11

The day Rebecca Vanderhall met her inevitable future dawned cold and bright. The brilliant sunlight, the achingly clear blue skies, were a clear representation of her happiness – and the happiness she was now confident awaited her.

It was Christmas Eve, and she was getting married.

Ethan waited for her at the foot of the stairs, his eyes searching hers anxiously.

"Are you sure about this?" he said. "We don't need to rush things. I'm happy to wait for as long as you need."

She smiled at him. It was impossible *not* to smile at him.

"I don't want to wait any longer," she said. "I know it sounds silly – we've only known each other a few weeks, after all. But I feel as though I've known you all my life. I feel as though I've been waiting for you all my life. Besides, the whole town was expecting a wedding to happen yesterday. They've already been disappointed once – we can't let them down again."

"Oh, they'd find other things to be disappointed by," Ethan said, grinning at her. "Besides, they can be entertained by a trial, for one thing."

"Do you think he'll go to trial? Suppose he tries to justify himself, talking his way out of it."

"You've met Walter Adams. Do you think that man could control his ego long enough to talk his way out of anything?"

She shook her head. "You're probably right. Well, I don't care about it anymore. All I care about is Mother and you."

"And all I care about is you and your mother. You see? We have so much in common. No wonder we're getting married today."

She reached out and took his arm and stepped off the last step onto level ground with him. With a smile that was positively devilish, he pointed upward.

Above their heads, newly tied in place, was a sprig of mistletoe.

Becky met his gaze staunchly. "Well, well," she said, teasing him. "Would you like to kiss your bride, Mr. Dowser?"

He pressed her.

"Nothing would make me happier, Miss Rebecca."

As he kissed her at last, Becky wondered when she had begun to consider "Miss Rebecca" as the most perfect expression of love and affection she'd ever heard.

She didn't wonder for long, however. Her mind quickly turned to the wonderful man who was kissing her.

The End

CONTINUE READING...

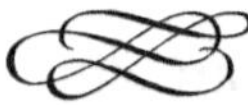

Thank you for reading *Christmas at the Inn!* Are you wondering **what to read next?** Why not read *Christmas in the Abandoned Farmhouse?* **Here's a peek for you:**

On December first, Margaret Jameston realized her twice-turned and much-mended coat was simply not going to last her another frigid Boston winter—it likely wouldn't even make it until Christmas.

She buttoned it tightly around her, but even with as many layers as she possessed, she would still feel the biting of the wind. The only part of her that ever stayed warm was beneath the thick woolen scarf wrapped three times around her neck, the ends tucked into the top of her coat – her mother's scarf, and one of the only pieces of Margaret's old life that still remained.

She sighed heavily, feeling like an unwanted house, falling down, with the wind coming in at the edges of the windows and whistling under the roof...

But maybe that was simply the power of suggestion, brought on by her surroundings. The little house next to the church where she was now living was ill-kept and drafty, and before she even set foot outside, she knew how cold it was likely to be. Mr. Eberhart, the preacher, found it difficult to maintain his house and keep food on the table. His salary was very small, and his family generously-sized, and seeming to grow every year.

There was a constant strain on the family, and Margaret also knew that her presence was not helping in the least. When she had agreed to come into the fold, so to speak, she had not counted on it being such a lengthy stay.

But now eight months had gone by, eight months of heartbreak and frustration, as she tried her best to move past the death of her beloved father, adjust to her sudden change in circumstances, and locate steady employment that would enable her to find lodgings elsewhere and care for herself.

Eight months of little to no result...

She was standing at the front window, looking out on the churchyard where her father lay, and steeling herself to venture into the cold when Lillian Eberhart came up to stand beside her, the baby in her arms.

Lillian was the second Mrs. Eberhart, scarcely five years older than Margaret herself. At twenty-five, she'd had two children of her own already with her husband, on top of taking care of the three that had already been in existence when she agreed to become the wife of the humble clergyman on the outskirts of Boston.

Visit HERE To Read More!

https://ticahousepublishing.com/mail-order-brides.html

ABOUT THE AUTHOR

Susannah has always been intrigued with the Western movement - prairie days, mail-order brides, the gold rush, frontier life! As a writer, she's excited to combine her love of story with her love of all that is Western. Presently, Susannah lives in Wyoming with her hubby and their three amazing children.

www.ticahousepublishing.com
contact@ticahousepublishing.com